Abney and Teal, how does it feel,

To live in the park on an island?

It's just right for us – it's adventurous!

And it's home, home on our island.

Text by Stella Gurney
Illustrations by Joel Stewart and Davide Arnone

First published 2013 by Walker Books Ltd
87 Vauxhall Walk, London SE11 5HJ

10 9 8 7 6 5 4 3 2 1

The Adventures of Abney & Teal © and ™ 2011 Ragdoll Worldwide Ltd.
Produced by Ragdoll.
Licensed by Ragdoll Worldwide Ltd.

This book has been typeset in AbneyandTeal font

Printed in China

British Library Cataloguing in Publication Data: a catalogue record
for this book is available from the British Library

ISBN 978-1-4063-4811-8

www.walker.co.uk

The Adventures of
ABNEY & TEAL

The Games Day

Joel Stewart

WALKER BOOKS
AND SUBSIDIARIES
LONDON · BOSTON · SYDNEY · AUCKLAND

It's a brisk, breezy morning in the park, just right for playing games. Abney and Teal are playing running-as-fast-as-you-can. And so are the Poc-Pocs.

poc!

pa-rump!

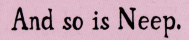

And so is Neep.

Neep!

They run and run until they fall down in
a bundle, giggling and panting.

"Well, we've done running," says Abney.
"Now what shall we play?"

"Let's play towers!" says Abney.
"Good idea!" cries Teal. So she collects
lots of useful things from outside.

Tra
la la

And Abney looks inside for more things too.

Hmm, what else?

And then they use their things
to build the tallest towers they can.
Whoops! Teal's tower is starting
to wobble!

Nearly there!

Neep!

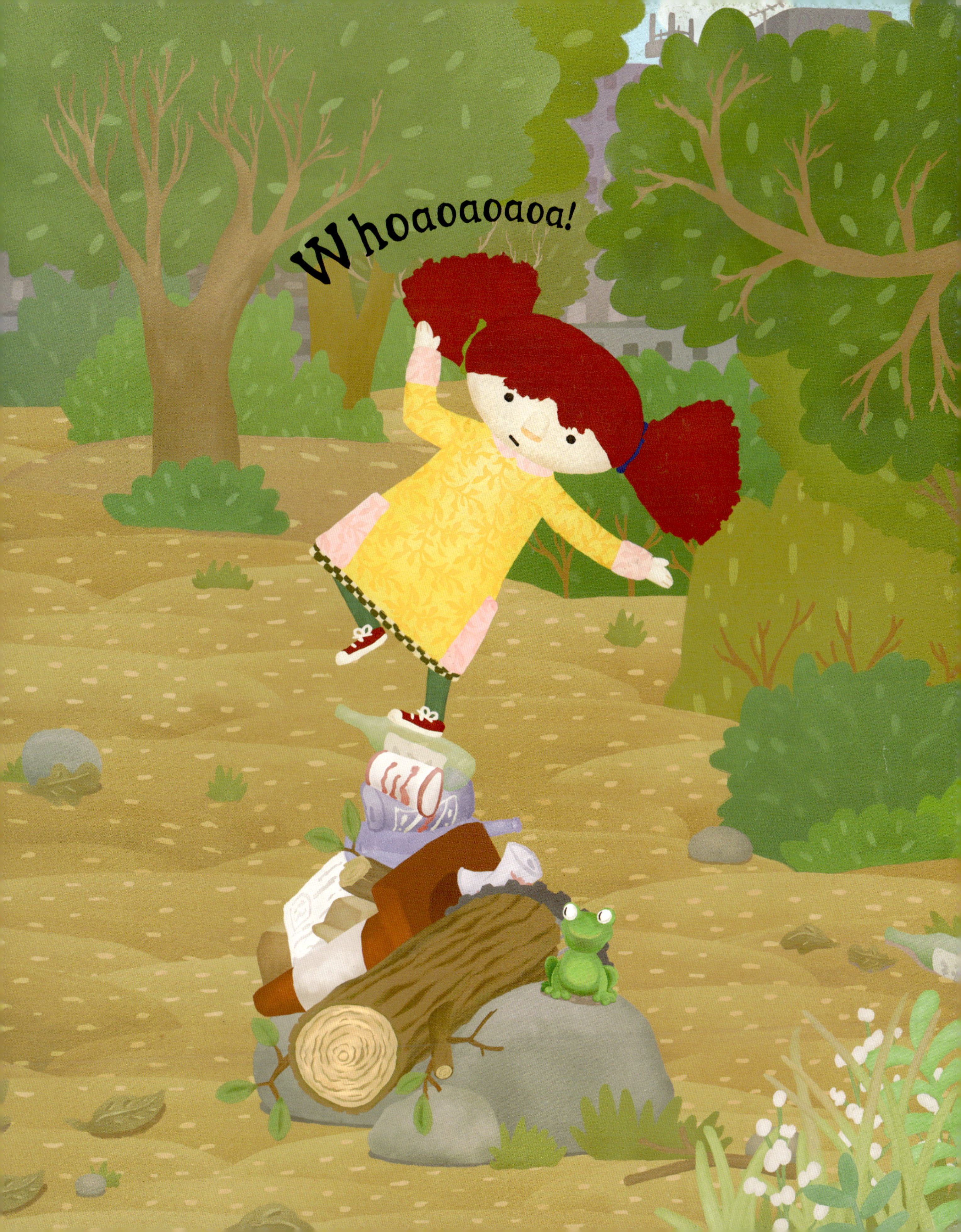
Whoaoaoaoa!

"Wow!" says Teal, swinging from the tree.
"That was brilliant!"
"It looks quite high up there, Teal," says Abney.

"Let's play a swinging
game!" calls Teal.
"Catch hold of my hands,
and I'll pull you up!"

"Oh – are you sure?"
says Abney.

Whoops!
Teal has let go of Abney's hands.

"My goodness!" says Abney as he lands in a pile of leaves. "I think I need a rest now!" But Neep is ready to start a new game. He dives down into the earth.

"Let's play your digging game, Neep!" says Teal. Everyone joins in. Even Abney has a go after his little rest.

After a while, Abney notices something.
"The Poc-Pocs are playing hide-and-seek!
Where are they?" he asks Teal.

Poc-Pocs!

Poc-Pocs!

Poc-Pocs!

Poc-Pocs!

"Oh dear," says Abney. "I hope they're all right.
The sun is starting to go down and it will be dark soon."

cheep
cheep

"There you are, Poc-Pocs!" laughs Teal.
"Clever old Neep! He found you! Well, I enjoyed
that hide-and-seek game," says Abney.

poc

cheep!

"I think we all deserve a prize for how well we've done in our games," announces Teal. "Let's make everyone a medal," says Abney.

Yippeee string!

And so, tired out from their games, Abney and Teal and Neep and the Poc-Pocs all have a lie-down in the setting sun, while Toby Dog plays them a tune from across the water. "That was an adventure, wasn't it, Abney?" murmurs Teal. But Abney is fast asleep.

ZZZZZZZZZZZ

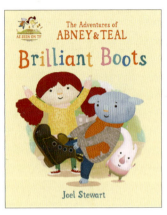

The Adventures of
ABNEY & TEAL
Other books from Abney and Teal:

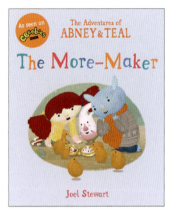

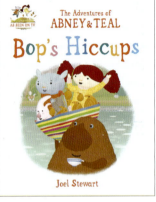

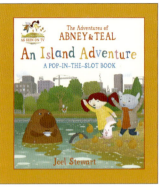

ISBN 978-1-4063-4490-5   ISBN 978-1-4063-4421-9   ISBN 978-1-4063-4491-2   ISBN 978-1-4063-4812-5

Abney and Teal toys also available:

ABNEY & TEAL MIX & MATCH CARD GAME

ABNEY & TEAL BEAN TOY ASSORTMENT

ABNEY & TEAL 24 PIECE FLOOR PUZZLE

"neep neep"

"neeeep"

ABNEY & TEAL WOODEN DOMINOES

ABNEY RAG DOLL

TEAL RAG DOLL

TALKING NEEP PLUSH